Lost in the Maze

written by Jay Dale

illustrated by Amanda Gulliver

"Look!" said Dad.
"Here is the maze."

"I will hide
inside the maze," said Lea.
"You can come after me."

"1, 2, 3, 4, 5.
I am coming to get you!"
shouted Dad.

Dad went into the maze.
He went up and down.

"Lea!" shouted Dad.
"Where are you hiding?
I am looking for you."

"I am hiding
inside the maze!"
shouted Lea.
"I like hiding.
It is fun."

Lea went up and down
the maze.
She did not stop.
She ran and ran.

"Oh, no!" cried Lea.
"I am lost!"

"Stop!" shouted Dad.
"Stop where you are.
I will look for you."

Lea stopped.
She did not run
up and down the maze.

"Dad!" cried Lea.
"Can you see me?
I am lost."

"Here I am!" said Dad.